Rabbit's Party

Written by Eve Bunting • Illustrated by Ellen Sloan-Childers

SCHOLASTIC INC.

New York   Toronto   London   Auckland   Sydney

Copyright © 1994 by Scholastic Inc.
All rights reserved. Published by Scholastic Inc.
Printed in the U.S.A.
ISBN 0-590-27386-8

2 3 4 5 6 7 8 9 10   08   00 99 98 97 96 95 94

"Tomorrow is my birthday,"
Rabbit said to himself. "I think I will
give a party."

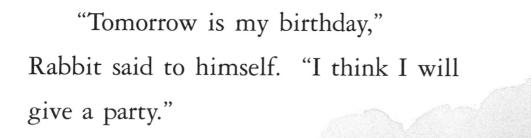

Then Rabbit thought, "But I only have three friends. A party won't work with only three friends."

Rabbit thought hard. "I know.
I will ask each of my friends to bring
two friends. Then there will be ten
of us at my party. What a good plan."

Rabbit went up to his
friend Squirrel.

"Do you know what?
Tomorrow is my birthday.
Please come to my party
and bring two friends."

"Thank you," Squirrel
said. "We will come."

Rabbit went up to his
friend Frog.

"Do you know what?
Tomorrow is my birthday.
Please come to my party
and bring two friends."

"Thank you," Frog
croaked. "We will come."

7

Rabbit went up to his
friend Mouse.

"Do you know what?
Tomorrow is my birthday.
Please come to my party
and bring two friends."

"Thank you," Mouse
squeaked. "We will come."

Rabbit was happy. He went home
and got ready for his party.

He made a nut cake with sweet berries
on top. "Yum," Rabbit said. "So good."

He made a big salad with carrots in it.
"Yum, yum," Rabbit said.

The next morning, Rabbit waited
for his guests. He saw Squirrel and Frog
and Mouse coming together.

"Where are your two friends?" Rabbit asked Squirrel.

"Here they are," Squirrel said. "I brought Frog and Mouse."

"Goodness me!" Rabbit said. "What a thing!"

"Where are your two friends?" Rabbit asked Frog.

"Here they are," Frog croaked. "I brought Squirrel and Mouse."

"Goodness me!" Rabbit said. "What a thing!"

"Where are your two
friends?" Rabbit asked Mouse.

"Here they are," Mouse
squeaked. "I brought Squirrel
and Frog."

"Goodness me!" Rabbit
said. "What a thing!"

Rabbit and his friends sat
at the table.

"Everything is so good,"
Squirrel said.

"What a great party!" Mouse
squeaked. "I like the nut cake."

They all liked the nut cake.

Rabbit looked around the table.

"I found out something today," he said.

"Three good friends are enough. A party will

work with just three friends."

"Indeed! Please pass the nut cake," Mouse said.